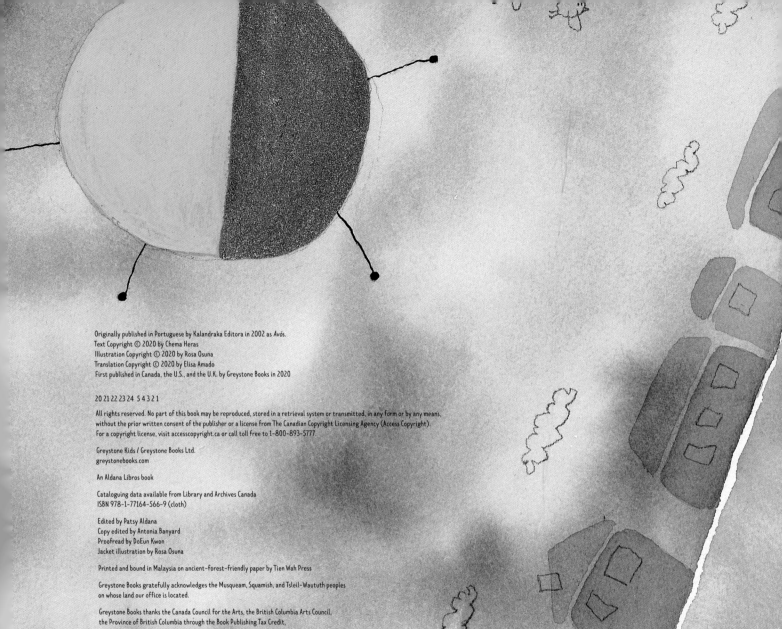

Originally published in Portuguese by Kalandraka Editora in 2002 as *Avós*.
Text Copyright © 2020 by Chema Heras
Illustration Copyright © 2020 by Rosa Osuna
Translation Copyright © 2020 by Elisa Amado
First published in Canada, the U.S., and the U.K. by Greystone Books in 2020

20 21 22 23 24   5 4 3 2 1

Greystone Kids / Greystone Books Ltd.
greystonebooks.com

An Aldana Libros book

Cataloguing data available from Library and Archives Canada
ISBN 978-1-77164-566-9 (cloth)

Edited by Patsy Aldana
Copy edited by Antonia Banyard
Proofread by DoEun Kwon
Jacket illustration by Rosa Osuna

Printed and bound in Malaysia on ancient-forest-friendly paper by Tien Wah Press

Greystone Books gratefully acknowledges the Musqueam, Squamish, and Tsleil-Waututh peoples
on whose land our office is located.

Greystone Books thanks the Canada Council for the Arts, the British Columbia Arts Council,
the Province of British Columbia through the Book Publishing Tax Credit,
and the Government of Canada for supporting our publishing activities.

Canada

Canada Council   Conseil des arts
for the Arts   du Canada

BRITISH COLUMBIA   BRITISH COLUMBIA ARTS COUNCIL
An agency of the Province of British Columbia

GRANDPARENTS

BY Chema Heras · ILLUSTRATIONS BY Rosa Osuna · TRANSLATED BY Elisa Amado

AN ALDANA LIBROS BOOK

GREYSTONE KIDS

GREYSTONE BOOKS · VANCOUVER/BERKELEY

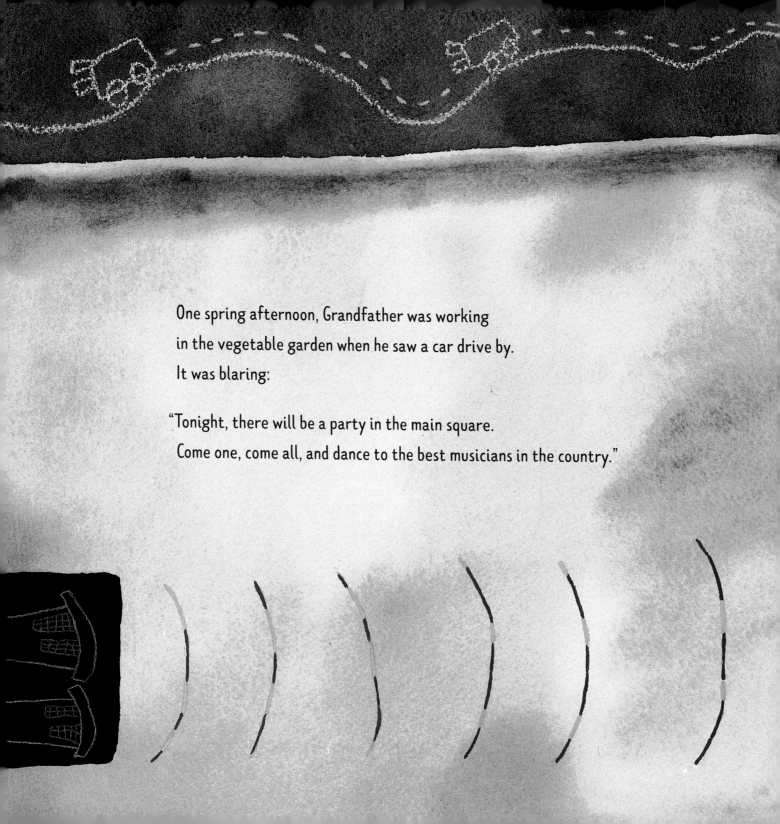

One spring afternoon, Grandfather was working
in the vegetable garden when he saw a car drive by.
It was blaring:

"Tonight, there will be a party in the main square.
Come one, come all, and dance to the best musicians in the country."

"Did you hear, Manuela? We have a dance tonight!"

"Yes, Manuel, but I'm not going.
I'm not flitting from party to party
like a girl anymore."

Grandfather said nothing.

He looked at the sun, which was
about to hide behind the horizon . . .

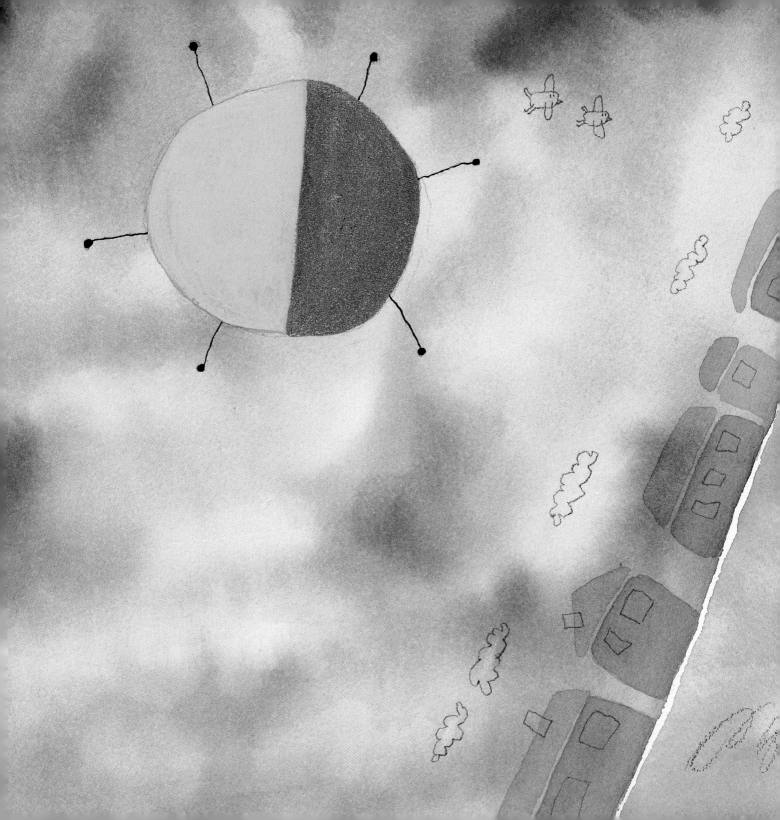

and bent over to pick a daisy that was growing in the grass.

Then he went to where Grandmother was, gave her the flower, and said, "But you are so pretty, Manuela. As pretty as the sun!"

Grandmother smiled and went to the mirror to look at herself.

"That's not true. I am as ugly as a chicken with no feathers,"
she said, putting the daisy in her hair.

"Don't say that! You are as pretty as the sun.
Now please hurry up. We have to go dancing!"

Grandmother went into the bathroom
and pulled a pencil out of a pouch.

"What are you doing with that pencil?" asked Grandfather.

"I'm going to put eyeliner around my eyes.
They are as sad as a moonless night."

"Don't say that! You are as pretty as the sun.
And your sad eyes are like stars at night.

Now please hurry up. We have to go dancing!"

Grandmother smiled and picked up a little brush.

"What are you doing with that brush?"

"I'm going to put mascara on my eyelashes.
They are as stubby as a little fly's feet."

"Don't say that! You are as pretty as the sun
with your starry, sad eyes.
And your short eyelashes are like new-mown grass.

Now please hurry up. We have to go dancing!"

Grandmother smiled again and slid
a little pot out of the cabinet.

"What are you doing with that little pot?"

"I'm going to put some cream on my skin.
It's as wrinkled as a dry fig."

"Don't say that! You are as pretty as the sun
with your starry, sad eyes,
your new-mown-grass short eyelashes.
And your wrinkly skin is just like nuts in a pie.

Now please hurry up. We have to go dancing!"

Grandmother smiled again,
put down the pot, and pulled out a lipstick.

"What are you doing with that lipstick?"

"I'm going to put some shine on my lips.
They are as dry as a dirt road in the country."

"Don't say that! You are as pretty as the sun
with your starry, sad eyes,
your new-mown-grass short eyelashes,
your wrinkly skin just like nuts in a pie.
And your dry lips are like sand in a desert.
Now please hurry up. We have to go dancing!"

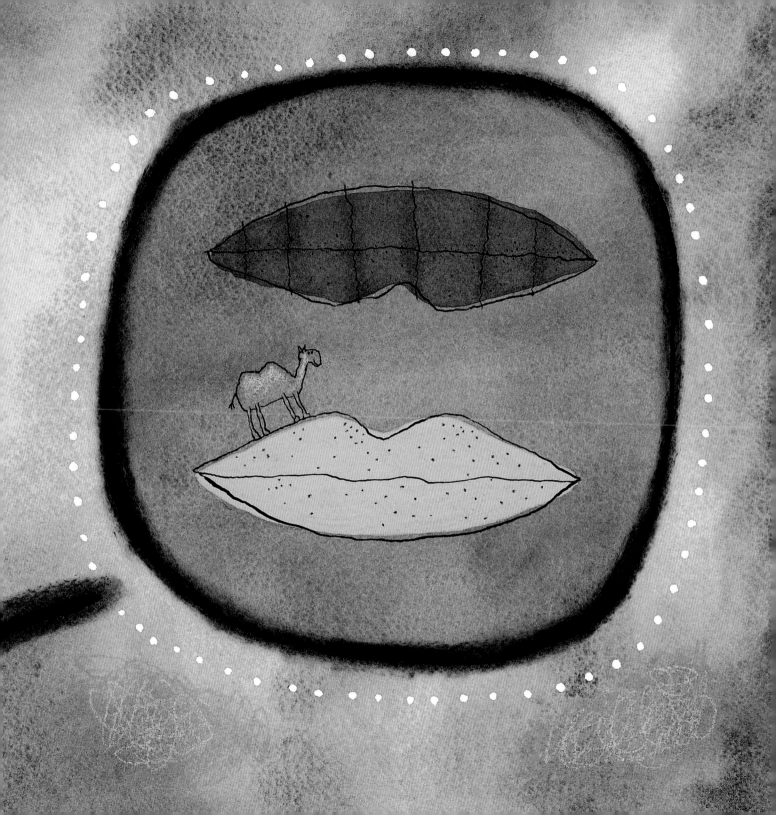

Grandmother smiled again,
went to the night table,
and got out a jar.

"What are you doing with that jar?"

"I'm going to dye my hair.
It's as gray as an autumn cloud."

"Don't say that!
You are as pretty as the sun
with your starry, sad eyes,
your new-mown-grass short eyelashes,
your wrinkly skin just like nuts in a pie,
your desert-sand dry lips.
And your white hair is like a midsummer cloud.

Now please hurry up. We have to go dancing!"

Grandmother smiled again, went over to
the wardrobe, and pulled out a skirt.

"What are you doing with that skirt?"

"I'm going to hide my legs.
They are as skinny as knitting needles."

"Don't say that! You are as pretty as the sun
with your starry, sad eyes,
your new-mown-grass short eyelashes,
your wrinkly skin just like nuts in a pie,
your desert-sand dry lips,
your white hair like a midsummer cloud.
And your legs are as skinny as a swallow's.
Now please hurry up. We have to go dancing!"

Grandmother folded up her skirt, washed her face, and smiled in the mirror.

Then she took Grandfather's arm, and together, they went to the dance.

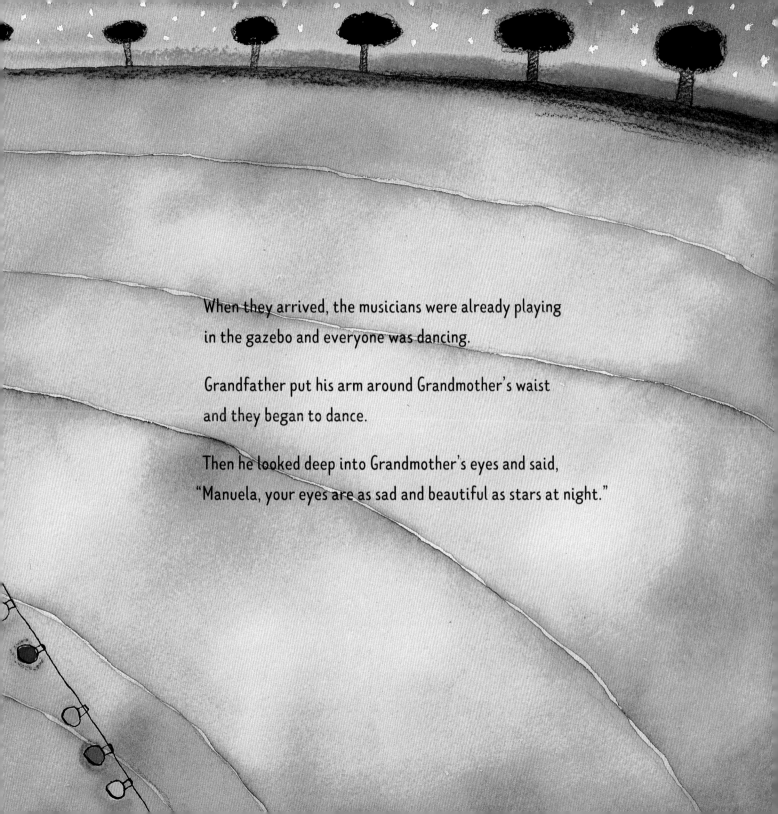

When they arrived, the musicians were already playing
in the gazebo and everyone was dancing.

Grandfather put his arm around Grandmother's waist
and they began to dance.

Then he looked deep into Grandmother's eyes and said,
"Manuela, your eyes are as sad and beautiful as stars at night."

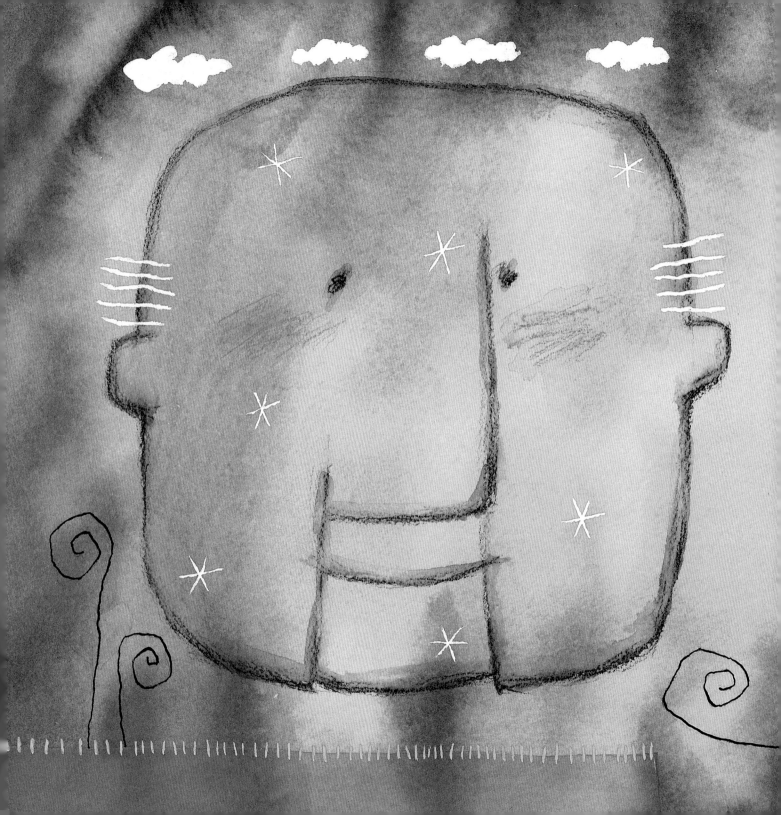

Then Grandmother looked deep into Grandfather's eyes

and saw that he, too, had sad eyes like stars at night,

short eyelashes like new-mown grass,

wrinkly skin just like nuts in a pie,

dry lips like sand in a desert,

white hair like a midsummer cloud,

and legs as skinny as a swallow's.

Grandmother bent down to pick a daisy
and pinned it to Grandfather's jacket.

She snuggled into his shoulder,
looked up at the sky,
then back into Grandfather's eyes,
and, without stopping dancing, said,
"Manuel, you are as pretty as the moon!"

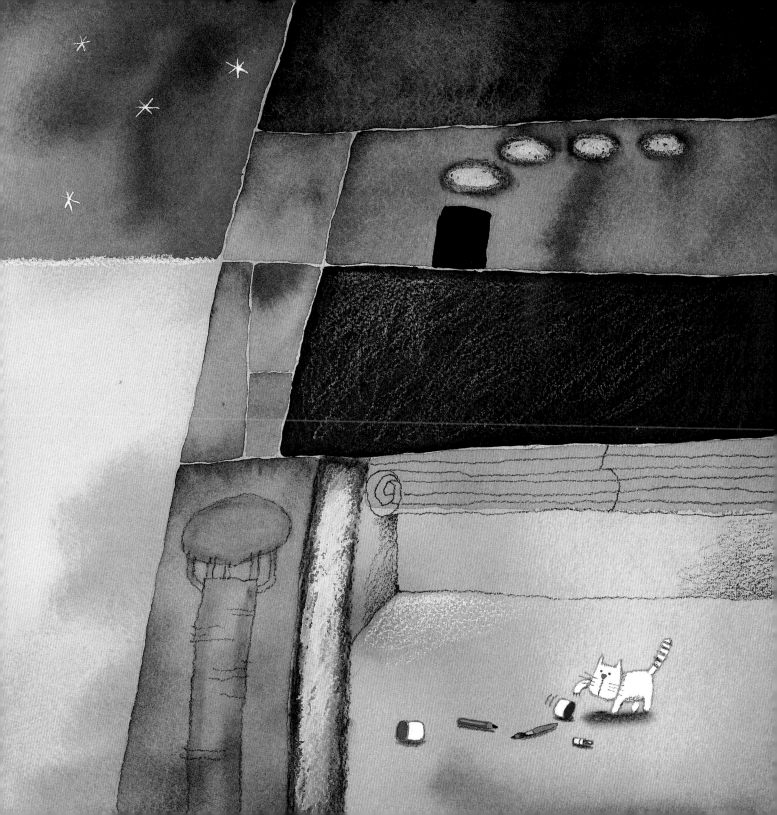